# A VERY NOISY GIRL

## BY
## ELIZABETH WINTHROP

## ILLUSTRATED BY
## ELLEN WEISS

HOLIDAY HOUSE/NEW YORK

*For Elizabeth Winthrop Alsop, who gave me the idea*

E. Winthrop


*For Mollie*

E. Weiss

Library of Congress Cataloging-in-Publication Data

Winthrop, Elizabeth.
A very noisy girl / by Elizabeth Winthrop Mahony :
illustrated by Ellen Weiss. — 1st ed.
p.   cm.
Summary: Elizabeth's mother gets a respite
from her very noisy girl
when Elizabeth pretends to be a dog.
ISBN 0-8234-0858-2
[1. Noise—Fiction.   2. Mothers and daughters—Fiction.
3. Imagination—Fiction.]   I. Weiss, Ellen, ill.   II. Title.
PZ7.W768Ve   1991      90-39175      CIP      AC
[E]—dc20
ISBN 0-8234-0858-2

Once there was a very noisy girl named Elizabeth.

She slammed doors

and jumped on furniture

and made loud slurping noises
when she ate her Cheerios.

"Elizabeth," her mother said. "Can't you be a
little quieter?"

But Elizabeth couldn't.
She pounded up and down the stairs

and turned cartwheels in the hall

and jumped over the umbrella stand.
"Elizabeth," her mother cried. "Stop making such a racket."

But Elizabeth couldn't. She played the piano and blew on her horn and beat her drums.

"Elizabeth," her mother shouted.

"Don't be such a noisy girl."

So Elizabeth went into her room and slammed the door.

When her mother called, "Elizabeth, it's time for lunch,"
Elizabeth came out of her room on all fours.

"Woof, woof," she barked.
"Who are you?" asked the mother.
Elizabeth didn't answer.

She sat up on her hind legs and held out one paw.
"Where is Elizabeth?" the mother asked. "What have you
done with my favorite girl?"

The dog barked and covered her eyes with her paws.

"Elizabeth," the mother called up the stairs. But there was no answer.

"Elizabeth," the mother called down the back hall. But still there was no answer.

Elizabeth was nowhere to be found. There was only a dog in the kitchen. The dog barked once and jumped up on Elizabeth's mother.

"You look like a very hungry dog," said the mother. "Since Elizabeth's gone, I might as well feed you her lunch."

So the mother cut Elizabeth's tuna-fish sandwich into tiny
little pieces. Then she set the plate on the floor.

The dog put her nose down and sniffed at the sandwich.
Then she nibbled it with tiny little quiet bites. She licked her
lips with her long pink tongue.

"Are you thirsty, Dog?" the mother asked. The dog barked again, so the mother poured the dog a bowl of milk and set it on the floor.

The dog lapped it up with small dainty licks.

Then she sat up on her hind legs and scratched her right ear.

"Let's go out in the garden," said the mother. "Now that Elizabeth's gone, I'll have some peace and quiet."

The mother sat in the sun and read a book. The dog curled up on the bench beside her and took a nap.

"Don't you want to swing on the swings?" the mother asked after a while.

"Elizabeth loves to swing. She pumps her legs up and down.

She swings high enough to see over the fence into the next yard."

The dog didn't answer.

"Would you like to jump rope?" the mother asked. "Elizabeth loves to jump rope. She can do fifty-four jumps without stopping. That's her record."

The dog opened one eye and closed it again.

"Why don't you climb the monkey bars?" asked the mother. "Elizabeth goes to the very top and plays King-of-the-castle. She stands up and waves at me, and I call to her to be careful but she doesn't pay any attention. Elizabeth is very brave."

The dog stood up, turned around and around in a circle and lay down again.

She went back to sleep.

The mother put down her book. "Dog, you're no fun at all.
I wish Elizabeth would come home again. It's much too quiet
here without her."

The dog sat up.

"Do you know where Elizabeth is hiding,
Dog? Won't you please go find her for me?"
the mother said. "I miss her."

The dog jumped off the bench and trotted
into the house.

The mother sat on the bench and waited. She waited for a very long time.

"Oh dear," she said in a loud voice. "It looks as if Elizabeth is never coming back."

"Here I am," cried a voice, and Elizabeth
ran into the garden.

"Elizabeth, where have you been? I missed you so much," her mother said. "While you were gone, a dog came to visit. She ate all your lunch and drank all your milk and took a long nap. She was a very quiet dog."

Elizabeth frowned.

"But she was very boring," said her mother. "Even though you're noisy, you're much more fun."

Elizabeth grinned.

Then she jumped off the bench,

turned two cartwheels

and landed in her mother's lap.